The Little Red Elf

Barbara Barbieri McGrath

Illustrated by Rosalinde Bonnet

Charlesbridge

With fond memories of Martha Alexander's
contributions to children's literature—B. B. M.

For Augustin and Martin—R. B.

Published by Charlesbridge
85 Main Street
Watertown, MA 02472
(617) 926-0329
www.charlesbridge.com

Library of Congress Cataloging-in-Publication Data
McGrath, Barbara Barbieri, 1954-
The little red elf / Barbara Barbieri McGrath ; illustrated by Rosalinde Bonnet.
p. cm.
Summary: In this version of "The Little Red Hen," set at the North Pole, a penguin and a hare
refuse to help an elf plant, grow, and decorate an evergreen tree but nevertheless expect to open
the presents found under its branches on Christmas Day.
ISBN 978-1-58089-236-0 (reinforced for library use)
[1. Folklore.] I. Bonnet, Rosalinde, ill. II. Little red hen. English. III. Title.
PZ8.1.M176Lm 2009
398.2—dc22
[E]
2008025340

Printed in China
(hc) 10 9 8 7 6 5 4 3 2 1

Illustrations done in acrylic paint and black ballpoint pen on acrylic special paper Clairfontaine (165-lb.)
Display type and text type set in Alex, designed by Bob Alonso for BA Graphics
Color separations by Chroma Graphics, Singapore
Printed and bound by Jade Productions
Production supervision by Brian G. Walker
Designed by Susan Mallory Sherman

THE PENGUIN

THE LITTLE RED ELF

WORK SHOP

THE REINDEER

THE HARE

Once upon a time, there was a reindeer, a penguin, a hare, and a little red elf. They all lived together in a comfy, cozy workshop.

The reindeer liked to snooze in the straw.

The penguin liked to relax in the bathtub.

The hare liked to hibernate by the hearth.

That left the little red elf to get all the workshop work done.

She swept the sawdust and boxed the bulbs.
She organized the tools.
She stirred the paint and untangled the lights.
She shoveled the path and checked the mail and polished the sleigh.

One day while she was filling the bird feeders, she came upon some pinecones. "Who will help me plant these pinecones?" asked the little red elf.

"Not I," said the reindeer.

"Not I," said the penguin.

NOT I !

?

"Did someone say something?" mumbled the hare.

LITTLE
PINE TREE

"Then I will," said the little red elf. And she did.

Soon a little pine tree began to push through the ground. "Who will help me water the pine tree?" chirped the little red elf.

"Not I," said the reindeer.
"No, thanks," said the penguin.

"ZZZZZZZZZzzzzz," snored the hare.

"Not a problem—I'll do it myself,"
said the little red elf.

Each morning the little red elf watered the pine tree.
She was delighted to see it grow straight and tall.

LITTLE
PINE TREE

Finally the pine tree was ready. The little red elf asked her friends, "Who will help me bring the tree into the workshop?"

"Not I," said the reindeer.

"Blub, blub," squirted the penguin.

"ZZZZZZZZZZZzzzzz," snored the hare.

"Well, I love being busy!" said the little red elf with the most positive of attitudes.

The little red elf got her shovel and dug and dug and dug. She lifted the tree into a bucket and carefully brought it into the workshop. When the tree was positioned just the right way, the little red elf asked, "Who will help me string the lights on the tree?"

"Not I," said the reindeer.

Not I!

"What's with all the questions?" said the penguin.

"Ten more minutes," grumbled the hare.

ZZZZ ZZZZZZ

"Then I'll handle it," said the little red elf.

After the lights were up, the little red elf grew tired.
"I don't suppose there's anyone here who might assist me in
putting ornaments on the tree?" she begged.

"Not I," said the reindeer.
"They float, don't they?" said the penguin.
"Who's there?" said the hare.

The little red elf took a deep breath.
"That's okay, I can do this!" she exclaimed.

Soon the workshop began to glow and sparkle.

"Oooooooooh," said the reindeer.

"Aaaaaaaaahhh," said the penguin.

"You missed a spot," said the hare, with one eye open.

"Now that I have your attention," the little red elf said with a smile, "who will help me put out milk and cookies?"

"Not I," said the reindeer.

"Why bother saying yes now?" said the penguin.

"I'm allergic," said the hare.

"No big deal," said the little red elf.

The next morning piles and piles of presents sat under the tree. Everyone was up very early, for a change. The little red elf raised an eyebrow, though her voice was as sweet as ever. "Who will help me open the presents?"

"I will!" said the reindeer.

"I will!" yelled the penguin.

"I want the big one!" screamed the hare.

With that, the little red elf put her hands out and shouted,
"STOP! I planted the tree. I watered the tree.
I brought the tree into the workshop. I strung the lights.
I decorated the tree. I put out the milk and cookies.
Now I'm going to open all the presents myself."

The reindeer, the penguin, and the hare stood very still.
They were shocked. Then they began to cry.

The little red elf put her hands down. "Oh, please don't cry!" she said.
"I'm sorry. Of course you can open the presents."

The reindeer, the penguin, and the hare dove into the gifts. Paper and ribbon flew through the air.

"What did you get?" asked the little red elf.

"Aaah . . . the perfect gifts for you! Thank you, Santa!" she said.